Kevin
goes
First

Kevin goes First

Hala Tahboub

CLARION BOOKS

An Imprint of HarperCollinsPublishers

Fox was the **first** one to see the ladder.

Alligator was second.

Soon Horse showed up,
then Top Duck.
Then Pig.

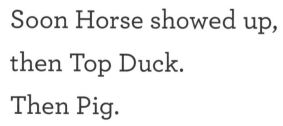

And before long, all the friends had gathered to
have a look at the ladder, including Kevin.

What's up there? they wondered.
Everyone was curious and there
was only one way to find out.

"I will go **first**," announced Kevin.

"I call caboose,"
said Horse.
"I like to go last."

"Second to last," said Pig.

"Third to last," said Alligator.

"I will stay, or maybe I won't," said Top Duck.

"We want to be **first**," Fox whispered to Gorilla.
"What if there's a strawberry donut up there?

"If Kevin gets up there **first**, he's going to eat the strawberry donut," said Fox.

"Remember when he took the **first** peek inside the treasure box?

"And when he was the **first** to press the magic button?

"And when he got to take the **first** bite of my freshly baked, straight-from-the-oven *strawberry* cake?

"Besides, I saw the ladder **first** and—"

But Kevin had already
started to climb.

"Winners go **first**," he said.

"I'm winning."

Kevin pulled himself higher and higher,
and a little higher than he'd liked.

He made it to the top before any of his friends.

Which meant that Kevin was alone,
but he did not mind.

Until he met Mouse,

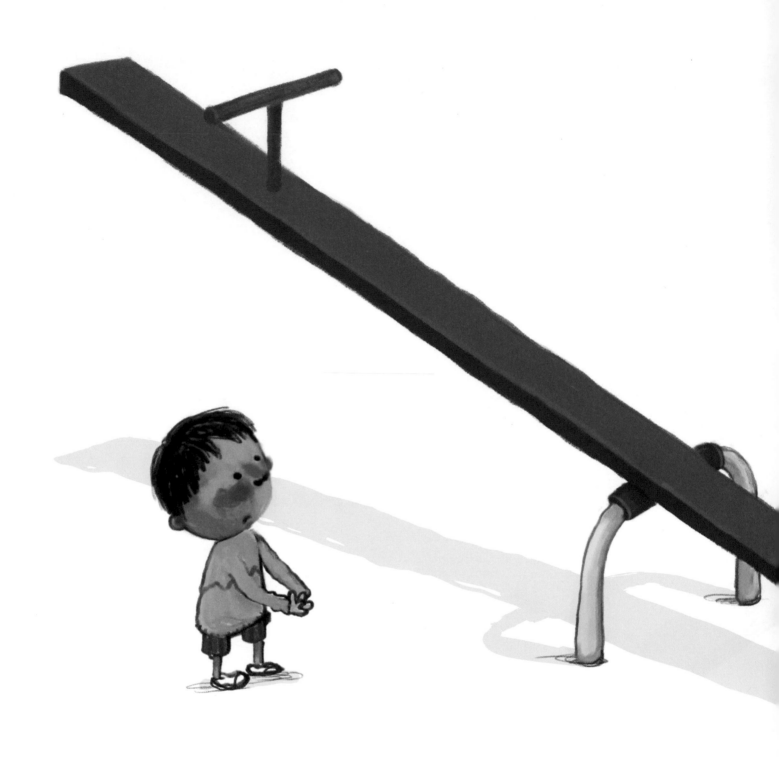

who was VERY excited to play with him.

It turned out Kevin was not
the **first** one up there . . .

But he was the **first** one to call for friends.

Kevin was also the **first** one
to celebrate their arrival . . .

. . . and Kevin was the very **first** one to get on second.

Which meant . . .

. . . he was the **first**

to see the strawberry donuts.

For Samir, Maha, Jumana, Rebecca, and Kait.

Clarion Books is an imprint of HarperCollins Publishers.

Kevin Goes First
Copyright © 2023 by Hala Tahboub
All rights reserved. Manufactured in Italy. No part of this book may be used or reproduced in any manner whatsoever without written permission except in the case of brief quotations embodied in critical articles and reviews. For information address HarperCollins Children's Books, a division of HarperCollins Publishers, 195 Broadway, New York, NY 10007.
www.harpercollinschildrens.com

Library of Congress Control Number: 2022044841
ISBN 978-0-06-325419-0

The artist used digital media to create the illustrations for this book.
Design by Phil Caminiti and Kevin
23 24 25 26 27 RTLO 10 9 8 7 6 5 4 3 2 1

first Edition